Boys
9–11 years

75p

MICHAEL AND THE
MOONSHINERS

MICHAEL AND THE MOONSHINERS

by
CHRIS WOOD

KINGSWAY PUBLICATIONS
EASTBOURNE

ISBN 0 86065 045 6

Printed in Great Britain for
KINGSWAY PUBLICATIONS LTD.,
Lottbridge Drove, Eastbourne, E. Sussex BN23 6NT
by Fletcher & Son Ltd,
Norwich

CONTENTS

CHAPTER ONE

MICHAEL WONDERS WHY

Life was hard in Cornwall two hundred years ago. It was specially hard in the small fishing village where Michael Trevane lived. Michael knew only too well what it was to be hungry. That was mostly when the fish were too cunning to be caught and the haul was a pitiful reward to the men who risked their lives battling with the wind and waves to pull in their near-empty nets.

Michael could remember enough of his early childhood to know that things were different if you happened to be rich. Then you owned a tin mine, or rich pasture land where you could grow crops or keep sheep and cattle. Michael's grandfather had owned a flourishing quarry where the granite fetched a good price. But times had changed.

Nowadays Michael's father worked the same quarry, but he did not make much money from it because someone else had opened up a bigger quarry with better equipment on the other side of the Downs. Not only had the new quarry taken most of Mr. Trevane's business away, but it had taken his best workmen as well. Now the Trevanes were almost as poor as the fishermen among whom they lived. If their neighbours envied them at all it was only because they owned a donkey and had a small back yard to keep her in.

Michael knew what it was to be cold as well as hungry. It was a bitter winter and his shirt and cloak were threadbare and little protection against the fierce gales that swept up the narrow village street. Sometimes the wind tore the slates off the tiny cottage roofs.

"And it's doing its best to rip the shirt off my back as well," Michael complained to his mother one particularly wild day.

"Well hang onto it a bit longer, lad. Maybe you'll have a new one soon," his mother said.

Michael flung his bare arms across his chest and beat himself hard on the shoulders, smiling ruefully at his mother as he did so.

"Poor Mum, the holes in your shawl look as if they let a rare old gale in too," he said.

"Never mind, I'm sure I'll have a new one before winter's done," she said, yet Michael could not see how that was likely.

But in spite of the hardships Michael was a happy boy. He was strong and healthy, with black windswept hair and dark, twinkling eyes. His mother said he was happy because he was not afraid of hard work. She worked hard too, doing what she could to make ends meet by selling cheese, and weaving cloth on a quaint old loom.

One of Michael's jobs was to sell his mother's cloth in Helston, a small market town some eight miles away. He loved going across the Goonhilly Downs to Helston. It gave him a chance to visit his cousins Trevor and Elizabeth, and when he came home his head always buzzed with the latest news hot from the market place.

8

One morning when Michael tumbled out of his straw bed he remembered he was going to the market that day, and he was thrilled about it. A whole month had passed since he last went.

"Before you set off with my cloth I want you to go down to the beach and get some driftwood," his mother said. "Last night's storm should have washed plenty ashore and we're almost out of firewood."

Really Michael should have gone straight down the narrow street to the beach, but he preferred a longer route to a tiny, hidden cove. He climbed a rough track leading onto the cliff that towered above the village like a gigantic sentinel. It was hard going, especially as Michael had the wind against him all the way, but it would take a tougher climb than that to make a boy like Michael out of breath.

When Michael reached the cliff top he found the wind blowing even more strongly but it did not bother him. He raced along, his cloak flying out behind him, like a fox fleeing from a pack of hounds. He did not stop until he came to another, more twisty path leading down to the small cove which was cut off from the main beach by a massive fall of rock.

Not many people knew about this path and even fewer used it. Michael liked to think he shared his secret only with the seagulls and a few of the younger fishermen.

He jumped the last few feet onto the sand and stood with his back against the cliff. The wind blew full in his face, making his eyes smart and his hair stand on end. As he stood there, Michael listened to the exciting thunder of the waves as they pounded against a

9

ridge of cruel rocks further out to sea. These rocks were known locally as the Devil's Teeth and, as Michael well knew, seafarers had every cause to fear them. He shuddered as he recalled some of the valiant ships that had met their doom in these fiendish, merciless jaws.

"The sooner you grind those teeth down the better," Michael shouted to the mighty waves, then he turned and went into his favourite cave. Michael had always liked this particular cave. He was fascinated by the way it opened out into a vast cavern. There was a narrow crack in the vaulted roof and it was just enough to let a shaft of daylight through and make exploring that much easier.

"This is the sort of cavern where you'd expect to find anything from a seal to a seaman's chest," Michael said, and his voice echoed eerily from the vaulted roof. "The trouble is I never do find anything," he added with a shrug.

But that was where Michael was wrong. In the dim light he suddenly noticed something on a rocky ledge, something he was quite sure had never been there before. He reached up eagerly and lifted it down. To his surprise it was a lantern, not a rusty old thing that could have been washed up by the tide, but a proper lantern in full working order. Michael knew it was just the sort of lantern that anyone in the village would use.

"But how in the world did you get in here?" Michael asked with a puzzled frown.

And he was annoyed as well as puzzled. He did not like the idea of anyone but himself coming to this particular cave. It had been his secret den for as long as he could remember and if anyone put anything there it should, he felt, be him.

Michael replaced the lantern on the ledge, still wondering who had left it there and why. He groped his way back to the mouth of the cave and looked for footprints in the sand but, apart from his own, there were none. The tide had washed away any tell-tale clues.

For the first time ever Michael was glad to be out of that cave. All at once it had become a creepy place with a secret that he did not share. Michael shivered uneasily, and yet he could not tell why he should feel so uneasy. After all lanterns were harmless enough things—or were they?

A broken plank lying nearby reminded Michael with a start that he was supposed to be collecting driftwood. He picked up the plank and went on collecting bits and pieces until he had as much wood as he could carry. As he left the cove he glanced once more towards his favourite cave.

"It's queer but I *know* that lantern shouldn't be there," he muttered. And he went on thinking about it as he struggled to the cliff top with his load of wood.

Michael meant to tell his mother about the lantern when he got home, but she was cross with him for being so long and he did not have a chance.

"Have you forgotten you're going to Helston to-day?" she asked. "Hurry and spread that wood in the fender, then off you go. Market will be over by the time you get there if you don't get a move on."

Michael quickly spread the driftwood out to dry,

11

then ran into the back yard to harness Nellie the donkey. He also fastened two large baskets to her sides, then led her to the cottage door. Mrs. Trevane lost no time in filling the baskets with the cloth she had woven.

"Off you go," she said, "and don't dawdle about on those Downs. They're no place for a boy like you to hang around on, as I've told you before . . . and be sure you're back before dark. . . ."

"What about something to eat?" Michael interrupted.

"Food! That's one thing you never forget," said his mother with a smile. Michael was glad to see her smiling because she had been unusually abrupt up to then as if something was bothering her—something more serious than Michael staying too long on the beach.

Mrs. Trevane hurried into the cottage and soon returned with some cheese, a chunk of barley bread and an apple.

"Have you packed all the cloth you've woven?" Michael asked. "Only there's usually a lot more than this."

"You'll be lucky to sell that much this late in the day," his mother replied.

"But usually both baskets are crammed full," Michael persisted.

"Do hurry up and stop arguing," said his mother sharply.

Michael shook his head in bewilderment and set off with a worried look in his usually twinkling eyes.

"It's queer," he thought, as he led Nellie up the

narrow road that led past his father's quarry to the Downs. "There's definitely not as much cloth to sell as usual. Come to think of it, Mum doesn't sit up weaving late at night the way she used to do, and yet we haven't been so hard up lately. We have more food to eat and Mum said I might even have a new shirt before long. . . ."

Once again Michael shivered and felt uneasy. It was the same foreboding sort of feeling that had come over him when he discovered that lantern in his favourite cave.

CHAPTER TWO

UNWELCOME NEWS

Michael walked quickly and the laden donkey trotted eagerly beside him. Nellie enjoyed nothing more than a day out with Michael. It suited her far better than dragging heavy loads to and fro in Mr. Trevane's dusty old quarry.

Soon the village was left behind, hidden in the hollow between two huge outcrops of rock. As Michael approached the entrance to the quarry he paused, hoping to wave to his father as he passed. But the only person in sight was an old man with a bent back who was hewing away at a block of granite as if his life depended on getting it exactly the right size and shape. The old man was so intent on his task that he did not even look up when Michael called out to him.

"The men must be working on the rock face at the far end of the quarry," Michael told Nellie, but she did not want to know anything about the granite works and flicked her ears impatiently.

On up the rough track they went until they reached more even ground and Michael took in deep breaths of the crisp air of the wild Goonhilly Downs.

"Let's hope it won't be misty when we come back, Nellie," Michael said. "It's a menace the way fog can come in at the turn of the tide. Then you can't see a thing up here."

Nellie lifted her head and blew down her nose.

14

Then she twitched her long ears again and trotted on gaily. It was plain that she did not believe in worrying about sea fogs or any other troubles until they were actually upon her. But Michael had been caught in a thick mist before and it had been a wide-awake nightmare trying to find his way home.

"Oh goodness, I've forgotten the lantern!" Michael suddenly exclaimed. "Too late to turn back now so it just mustn't turn foggy, that's all."

Yet Michael could not understand how he had come to forget the lantern. It hung on a nail outside Nellie's shed and you could not miss seeing it.

"Now I come to think of it, I'm positive it wasn't there . . . or am I only making excuses for myself?" Michael said.

Since going back was out of the question, Michael cheered himself with the thought that it was not likely to become foggy while such a strong wind blew. He drew his thin cloak more closely round him and hurried on. He had crossed several miles of downland before the welcome sight of a church tower came into view.

"We'll soon be there now, that's the church near the market square," Michael said and Nellie quickened her pace as the rough track took on a downward slope.

Michael found the town as crowded as it always was on market day and trade was brisk. Pigs, sheep, geese and cattle changed hands quickly. Michael chose a spot beside a pottery seller to display the cloth he had come to sell and it was not long before he had his first customer. The material Mrs. Trevane wove always sold well, she was a skilled weaver and her cloth smooth and even. By early afternoon Michael had sold out.

"There now, I could have sold twice as much if only Mum had made it. I wonder why. . . ."

Michael's thoughts were interrupted by the sound of running feet and excited shouting. The potter hastily packed his few remaining wares, grumbling as he did so.

"What's happening?" Michael asked him.

"It's that preacher man, I'll be bound. Draws the crowds like a magnet, he does. For all that there's many in these parts who don't want to hear him. If he values his skin he would do better to stay away."

"You mean he preaches right here in the market place?" Michael asked.

"For sure he does. Look, what did I tell you? That's him on horseback—the great Mr. Wesley himself."

Michael thought 'great' an odd word to describe such a small, wiry man but did not say so. He had only heard vaguely of Mr. John Wesley, and yet the excitement of the jostling crowd was infectious and Michael became excited too. He was about to push his way into the throng when someone grabbed him by the arm.

"Mike! At last we've found you! We've looked everywhere for you, haven't we Beth?"

Michael turned to see his cousins Trevor and Elizabeth grinning at him.

"Yes, we looked for you all the morning," Beth added, with a twirl of her skirts.

"I didn't get here until mid-day because . . ."

"Come on, or we shan't get a good place at the front," Trevor interrupted. "You must hear Mr.

Wesley preach."

Michael and his cousins pushed their way through the crowd and stood by a water-trough close to where Mr. Wesley had dismounted from his horse. Michael was awe-struck by the masterly way the preacher held up his hand for silence and even more awe-struck by the expectant hush that immediately followed. You could have heard a winkle fall among the waiting market folk.

Michael had not heard a preacher since he went to church as a small boy, and he listened eagerly. John Wesley spoke simply yet powerfully of the true God who loved the world so much that He sent His Son to die in the place of sinful men.

"Many people don't believe on God's Son because they have never heard how He came to save them from their sins," the preacher said, "but, alas, there are many more who don't believe because they would rather carry on their wicked ways than come to Christ for forgiveness. Is anyone here today deliberately refusing God's gift of salvation through His Son?"

As John Wesley spoke it seemed to Michael that he looked straight at him. It was as if he knew there had been a time when God had a place in Michael's life, even though it was a long time ago. Michael did not hear much of the rest of the sermon. As he stood in the market place he recalled those far off days when his father had told him stories of Jesus, and how He died on a cruel cross to save all who believed on Him. Mr. Trevane had taught Michael to pray too and often knelt by his bedside with him.

In those days the Trevanes owned a horse as well as

17

a donkey and on Sundays his father would ride across the Downs to the church in this very town. He took his small son with him and now Michael recalled how much he had enjoyed riding between his father's legs, sometimes with only his face poking out from his father's thick winter cloak. He remembered too how quiet and holy the church seemed after the wind howling on the Downs and the clatter of the pony's hooves on the cobbled streets.

But then hard times came when the quarry no longer paid well and the pony had to be sold. Michael's father had ridden it to the market himself to be sure of finding a good master for the animal he was so loath to part with. When he had sold him he walked all the way home in the pouring rain.

After that the Trevanes stopped going to church and Michael forgot about God. Now he thought guiltily of how long it was since he last said his prayers.

Michael was jerked right back to the present as Mr. Wesley suddenly raised his voice. Never had Michael heard anyone speak with such authority.

"Even if you have forgotten God, or deliberately turned your back on Him, it's not too late to repent, not too late to ask God. . . ."

Suddenly there was an uproar from the back of the crowd and the rest of the sentence was lost. The next moment sticks and stones were hurled at the preacher and Michael and his cousins had to duck below the water-trough to avoid being hit. Eggs and potatoes followed, and then a lot of rotten apples came flying through the air.

The rough-looking men who started the trouble

18

forced their way to the front and tried to pull John Wesley from the stool on which he was standing.

"Repent, I say, it's not too late . . . not too late," the preacher shouted as eggs and stones rained fast, but the crowd listened no longer. They did not want to be involved in a riot and dispersed quickly.

Michael crouched beneath the water-trough and watched with pounding heart as a huge man with a flaming ginger beard shook his fist in Mr. Wesley's face.

"Get away from here and stop away . . . you won't be warned again, Mr. Preacher Man," he bawled.

"Yes, clear off. We don't want your pious talk," yelled another, and a general scuffle broke out as someone tried to make off with John Wesley's horse.

Michael dreaded to think how it might all have ended had not his uncle and three other respected citizens pushed forward and borne Mr. Wesley away by force. The preacher looked a sight with egg yolk dripping from his hair and cloak and yet he was plainly undaunted and moved with quiet dignity.

"Not too late! Not too late!" John Wesley's words were still ringing in Michael's ears as he crept from his hiding place and tried to wash some rotten apple from his cloak with the help of water from the trough.

"Come on, the market's not safe when those great louts are about," Trevor whispered, and Beth was so anxious to be off that she pulled Michael along by the hand.

"Wait a minute, I must get Nellie," Michael said, and hurried off to where the little donkey was tethered.

"It's a good job Daddy didn't see us hiding under that trough. He would be cross with us for coming here on our own," Beth said nervously, but once clear of the market she soon recovered her lively spirits.

"I wish our parson preached like Mr. Wesley," she said. "He makes everything so real."

"Perhaps it's as well he doesn't if it would mean being pelted with eggs and stones," Michael said, with a rueful grin.

"That's the trouble with Mr. Wesley, he makes things so real that people don't want to hear," Trevor replied. "Dad says it's because his words prick people's consciences and they know they ought to do what he says."

"That's not all," Beth added excitedly. "Do you know, Mike, there's lots of smugglers selling brandy and tea and things in this town and they're the ones who don't want to hear Mr. Wesley. He declares in front of everyone that smuggling's wrong because . . . because no duty is paid on smuggled goods and the Crown is robbed of its due."

Trevor burst out laughing at that.

"Honestly, Beth, the stuffy things you come out with," he said.

"But it's true, I heard Dad and Mr. Wesley talking about it last time he was here. And I know something else too," Beth said darkly. "I'm certain that horrid man with the ginger beard is the leader of a gang of moonshiners. It's him and his pals who always start trouble in the market place. Oh yes, he's a moonshiner all right and I hate him!"

"Stop using words like that, you know Dad's always

telling you about it," Trevor said sharply. "If you mean a smuggler, say so—but remember this. You can't accuse a man of cheating the Revenue Officers just because you don't like him. Things like that have to be proved."

"Well he looks like a moonshiner . . . a smuggler I mean, and his name's Rock Rufus, which is just the sort of name a smuggler would have," Beth persisted.

"I've never known anyone like you for finding things out," Trevor said, and now he sounded amused. "Is his name really Rock Rufus?"

"The trouble with you is that you don't *listen*," Beth replied. "And I'll tell you something else I know," she added, her eyes growing round with fear. "This morning I heard Daddy telling Mummy that smuggling will have to stop or it will ruin him. So many smuggled goods are being sold at half the proper price that Daddy will be forced out of business if it goes on . . . then we shall all die of cold and hunger."

Michael shuddered when he heard that. He knew far more about being cold and hungry than either Trevor or Beth could possibly know.

"Honestly Beth, how you do go on," Trevor said, and yet secretly he was as dismayed as Michael by this piece of news.

"Do you know what else I heard Daddy say? He said he can't afford to sell tea at less than ten shillings a pound because the duty is four and ninepence, yet other traders are selling it for five shillings a pound. They can do it because they dodge the duty by getting their tea off smugglers. Just think what will become of us when people won't buy Daddy's tea any more!"

Michael went on listening in troubled silence. Could the smugglers really reduce an honest merchant like his uncle to poverty? It did not bear thinking about. If it was true, whatever could be done to stop their illegal trading?

CHAPTER THREE

TROUBLE BREWS

Michael and his cousins turned a corner into a wide street where a few merchants' houses stood four storeys high on the other side of the road.

"There's Daddy, we've caught them up!" Beth exclaimed, and off she skipped to join her father and Mr. John Wesley.

"Mr. Wesley always visits us when he's in these parts," Trevor said. "Come in and have something to eat. It's fun listening to the tales he tells of his adventures up and down the country."

"I can't stop today, I've got to get home before dark," Michael replied.

That, of course, was true but Michael also wanted to be alone for a while. More than anything else he wanted to think over what the preacher had said about God sending His Son into the world to pay the price of sin.

"That must include all the wrong things I've done, as well as bigger things like smuggling and cheating the Customs Officers," Michael thought, "and it's not too late to tell God I'm sorry. That's what Mr. Wesley said—it's not too late."

"Isn't it queer the way things work out?" Trevor asked, interrupting Michael's thoughts. "Your dad gave up his chances of being a rich wool merchant to help Grandpa run his quarry. You've been pretty hard up since Grandpa died and we've been sorry for you all. Now, as Beth says, we may become poor ourselves with all this free trading in tea and sugar. If only the Revenue men could catch the smugglers when they're landing the stuff!'"

"Well they do sometimes, some were caught at St. Ives only last month. Bringing West Indian rum ashore they were," Michael said.

"How do you know?" Trevor asked.

"That old potter told me," Michael replied. "He said things are getting so hot for smugglers in St. Ives and even bigger places like Plymouth and Falmouth that they are trying to find new places to land their goods."

"Better mind they don't come to your village," Trevor said.

"Not much fear of that, it's such a tiny place. Anyway, the Devil's Teeth would put them off our bit of coast."

"Why don't you two come indoors instead of talk, talk, talk in the street?" Beth called from the doorway. "Hurry up, Mike, come and meet Mr. Wesley."

"No, I've got to go now. Perhaps he'll still be here next time I come to the market," Michael replied hopefully.

Then, with a wave to his cousins, he turned and hurried on his way. He knew he would have to move quickly to be home before dark. On the way Michael had plenty of time to think over the things he had heard that day. "It's not too late. It's not too late," Mr. Wesley's words still rang in his ears as he climbed the rugged track. And there, up on the lonely Downs,

Michael prayed his first prayer for a very long time.

"Please, God, forgive me for forgetting about You, and forgive me for all that I have done wrong," he prayed. "I know that Your Son, Jesus Christ, died that I might be forgiven—and I want to be a better boy and be a Christian like Mr. Wesley said. And, please God, don't let those smugglers ruin Uncle Arthur's business. Amen."

But, in spite of his prayer, the more Michael thought about smugglers, the more alarmed he became. If the Revenue men really had driven them from their usual haunts for landing contraband, surely more and more smuggled goods would find their way to the villages and towns on this part of the coast.

"There can't be much a boy like you can do to stop it, so you'll just have to go on asking God and trust Him to stop it," Michael told himself firmly, and after that he felt a little easier.

No sea fog blanketed the Goonhilly Downs that afternoon, but darkness began to fall when Michael was still some way from home. Nellie kept to the beaten track very well, but Michael could not help wishing it wasn't so eerie. Rocks and boulders took on strange shapes in the growing dusk and one jutting rock really made Michael jump. It looked exactly like a highwayman with pistol pointed at the ready.

"Not that you would get much out of me," Michael said to the offending rock, his voice sounding oddly high pitched and strained.

At last the salty tang in the air grew stronger and Michael knew he was nearly home. Nellie led the way unerringly down the track past Mr. Trevane's quarry, but when they neared the entrance she stopped abruptly. No amount of coaxing would move her on, she only bent her head lower and lower and became more and more obstinate.

And then the sound of a horse whinnying made Michael start. Who would be riding a horse at this time of the day, he wondered. He led Nellie back to where some large rocks offered a hiding place beside the path and slipped her reins over a tall, thin boulder.

"You stay here while I go and investigate," Michael whispered.

He crept cautiously towards the quarry entrance and what he saw made him gasp with astonishment. Not just one, but several horses were vaguely visible. To see horses in the quarry was puzzling enough but, even more bewildering, Michael could also see shaded lanterns flickering dimly as their owners moved swiftly to and fro.

Suddenly Michael was angry. Who were these men? Certainly they had no right in his father's quarry. No one ever went there after dark. The warning crunch of approaching hooves made Michael flatten himself against a large rock. A moment later a man came out of the quarry leading two ponies. Even in the semi-darkness Michael could tell that the ponies were heavily laden. Could it be that someone was stealing his father's granite?

Michael was so angry and frightened that he hardly knew what to do for the best. Should he run home and warn his father what was going on, or should he wait and watch? He was reluctant to go on without Nellie, but she was hidden further up the path, the way the ponies had gone. It would only take one bray to be-tray her presence and doubtless the thief, if thief he was, would think nothing of helping himself to a donkey.

"If only Nellie would come with me I could warn Dad of what's going on," Michael muttered, as he crept warily back to where the donkey was hidden.

But nothing would persuade Nellie to pass the quarry entrance until several more men, each leading two ponies, had gone and the place was left in com-plete silence and darkness.

"Crumbs, Nellie, I counted eighteen ponies go by," Michael said, as he rose from his hiding place under a projecting rock.

But the donkey was not interested. She set off down the track at such a pace that Michael stumbled and fell twice trying to keep up with her.

When they reached home Michael led Nellie round to the back of the cottage and reached for the lantern that hung by the shed door.

"Oh bother, it's not there. No wonder I forgot it this morning. What on earth has Dad done with that lantern?" Michael said impatiently.

With only fitful moonlight to help him, Michael put the donkey in her shed and made sure she was com-fortable for the night. Then he ran indoors, bursting to tell his father what he had seen at the quarry.

Mrs. Trevane often sat spinning beside the glowing range in the little back room, but tonight she was not there. In a way Michael was glad, he could go straight to his father with his news without the delay of being told off for being late home.

He hurried up the narrow passage leading to the front room, then stopped as abruptly as Nellie had done near the quarry. To Michael's surprise his parents had visitors, noisy men with loud voices. As he listened to the ribald laughter and clinking of mugs, Michael became more and more perplexed. These were the sort of noises he would expect to hear at the local tavern, but never in his own home. And he recognised some of the voices too. They belonged to tough villagers who had never had much time for the Trevanes, regarding them as 'foreigners' instead of fishermen born and bred like everyone else.

An extra loud laugh made Michael shiver. Only one man in the village laughed like that—Lobster Len, the toughest fisherman of all. His was a harsh, menacing laugh and Michael knew instinctively that it bode ill for someone when Lobster Len laughed like that. But for whom? And what was Lobster Len of all people doing in the Trevanes' cottage?

CHAPTER FOUR

THE UGLY TRUTH

"I'll be king of my own castle one day," Michael heard Lobster Len boast. "Mister Trevane here shall build it for me and I'll pay him a golden guinea for every stone he quarries, won't I? Ha! Ha! Gold he shall have ... gold ... gold ..."

Michael was strongly tempted to go on eavesdropping. It was, he knew, something Beth did with the greatest glee. She was a perfect terror for listening in on grown-up conversations, but Michael was old enough to know better. He dragged himself away from the door and went slowly back to the other room.

"Whatever's Lobster Len on about?" Michael whispered. "How could a poor fisherman possibly have a castle built for him? And even if he could, would he really let Dad quarry the stones to build it?

"He used to be dead against us," Michael added, remembering the time when Lobster Len had kicked him in the back for falling over a lobster pot.

All at once Michael realised how cold he was. He sat on the floor in front of the range and held out his hands to the friendly, warming glow. He had hardly sat down when the front room door opened, letting out a strong smell of rum and tobacco. This was the first time Michael's home had smelled of such things and he did not like it.

Michael looked up quickly as his mother came into

the little back room. She started when she saw him crouching on the floor.

"So there you are at last," she said nervously. "What do you mean by staying out so late? I've been worried sick about you alone on the Downs in the dark."

"Mum, I couldn't help being late. Something queer was going on at the quarry and I couldn't get past," and then Michael poured out the whole story of the flickering lanterns and laden ponies.

To Michael's dismay his mother collapsed into a rocking chair and covered her face with her hands.

"Mike. whatever happens you mustn't tell your father what you saw," she sobbed.

"Not tell him! Why not?"

"Because ... because he'd be very angry, that's why."

"You mean angry with me, or angry at what's going on?"

"I can't explain, lad, you wouldn't understand. Don't say anything, that's all."

"Of course I'd understand. Please tell me what's going on, Mum. For a start, what's Lobster Len doing in our house?"

But instead of replying, Mrs. Trevane began to sob more openly. Michael could not bear to distress her further by asking more questions, so he sat quietly for a while.

"Please don't be so upset, Mum. I didn't mean to be nosey," he said after a while. "Look, here's the money I got in the market today. I sold out ever so quickly, and then what do you think? I heard Mr. John Wesley preach. I expect you've heard of him, Trevor told me he travels hundreds of miles every year. He goes everywhere on horseback and preaches wherever he can."

"Oh yes, I've heard of Mr. Wesley, though I've never listened to him preaching," said Mrs. Trevane.

"Well, in the market he told us it's never too late to turn back to God no matter how wicked we've been. I haven't thought much about God for a long time, but up on the Downs I told Him I was sorry for all the wrong things I'd done and asked Him to make me a better boy."

"You? You're a right good boy as it is," Mum said, as she wiped away her tears. "You must be hungry after the long day you've had, I'll get you some supper."

Michael wanted to tell his mother how real God had seemed to him up there on the Downs, and how near too, but she began bustling to and fro and Michael could tell she was too busy to listen.

"There, eat that and then off to bed you go," she said, as she put Michael's supper on the table. "And remember, lad, not a word to anyone about what you saw at the quarry."

Usually Michael was so full of news that he could not stop talking when he came back from Helston, but tonight he munched his supper in silence. As soon as he had finished he climbed the ladder to his bed under the cottage rafters. It was a long time before sleep came to his eyes. The laughter and loud talk below did not help, and Michael wished he could hear what was being said without deliberately having to eavesdrop.

As he lay there, Michael tried to work out whether

there was any connection between the quarry mystery and the presence of Lobster Len and his friends in the cottage. If there was, what could the connection be? Once or twice horrid suspicions arose in Michael's mind, but he forced them away as being impossible.

"If only Mum would say something, or there was someone else to talk to," Michael wished. And then he remembered that there was Someone he could talk to at any time, Someone who was always ready to hear. And so for the second time that day Michael prayed, telling God how worried he was about the quarry and the noisy men drinking and shouting downstairs.

After that Michael felt a lot calmer and was quite sure God had heard him and understood far better than he did what was going on. And with that assurance he at last fell into a deep, untroubled sleep.

Had Michael known what plans were being made under the cottage roof that night, he would never have slept so soundly.

The next day dawned bright and clear and the fierce wind had dropped. Michael awoke to the sounds of hungry seagulls crying and the breaking of waves on the shore. He yawned and stretched, then lay on his back staring up at the dusty rafters overhead.

Suddenly he remembered his misgivings of the previous evening and sat bolt upright. He slipped noiselessly out of bed and pulled on his clothes. Then he went quietly down the ladder and into the front room.

Even in the early morning light a sorry sight met Michael's gaze. Empty mugs lay on their sides and the whole room was in disorder. Rum and stale tobacco fumes hung heavily on the air and Michael could not get the window opened fast enough. The fresh, salty air drove the last traces of sleepiness from him and he set about putting the room straight at once. His home, though humble, had always been neat and tidy and he could not bear to see it in such a muddle. As he stooped to retrieve a mug that had rolled under the table, something round and yellowish attracted Michael's attention. He picked it up and took it to the window.

"A gold coin! It's not a guinea but some foreign coin," he whispered. He turned it over and studied both sides carefully, but he could not tell what country the coin came from.

But of one thing Michael was quite sure. The coin did not belong to his father. That could only mean it belonged to one of the fishermen, but what would men like Lobster Len be doing with foreign money? And then Michael shuddered as he recalled Lobster Len's laugh and his loud boast that one day he would be king of his own castle.

"He told Dad he would pay him a golden guinea for every stone he quarried to build it," Michael said to a gaggle of geese who were waddling past the window.

Tidying up forgotten, Michael stayed by the window with his brow furrowed into a deep frown. It was no use trying to turn away from the truth any longer. Lobster Len and his friends must be in contact with countries across the channel. That, Michael knew, could only mean one of two things. Either they had gone in for free trading themselves or were in league with some smugglers, helping them to run contraband cargoes ashore.

"Whichever way it is, they obviously find it pays better than fishing for pilchards," Michael said with a grimace.

A more painful truth to be faced was the fact that his own father was in some way involved. Michael hated himself for believing such a thing, yet it did explain the extra food they had enjoyed recently and the promise of new clothes before long. It also explained why his mother no longer sat weaving until all hours of the night.

"She doesn't need to, there's money enough without it, money that's earned helping smugglers," Michael whispered, shivering the way he always did when he was ill at ease.

The more he thought about it, the more uneasy Michael became. How could he tell Trevor and Beth what he suspected. Only yesterday they had told him that free trading was ruining Uncle Arthur's business.

"How awful if Dad really is helping to put his own brother out of business," Michael thought. Of course his father would never do such a thing on purpose. Michael knew he would be horrified at the mere idea of it, but it could be sickeningly true all the same.

The more convinced Michael became that he had stumbled on the ugly truth, the greater his inner conflict became. He twisted the gold coin over and over in his hand, anguished by the thought that his father, who had first taught him to believe in God and all that was good, should have become mixed up with a bad thing like smuggling.

"I'll have to *do* something," Michael decided at

34

last, tossing the coin into the air. "But the question is, what?"

How could he openly accuse his own father? Michael loved him dearly and shrank from the very thought of such a thing.

At last Michael decided to do nothing for the time being. He knew there were Revenue Men in the Customs House at Falmouth who would be only too glad to hear of any smuggling haunts.

"But I'm not telling tales on my own Dad, that's one thing I'm certainly not going to do!" he said between clenched teeth.

Remembering how upset his mother had been the previous evening, Michael knew it would be a bad blunder to approach his father on the subject, too.

"What a jam I'm in!" he exclaimed.

He turned from the window and went into the back room to poke out the old range. He was about to re-light it when Mrs. Trevane joined him.

"You're up early, lad," she said. "I reckoned you were still asleep."

"I've been up ages making the front room tidy," Michael replied. "I should think those men might have picked up the chairs they knocked over, clumsy lot."

He wanted to tell his mother about the gold coin he had found but was afraid of upsetting her again. It was, he decided, wiser to say nothing about it.

After breakfast Michael went out to feed Nellie. The first thing he noticed was that the lantern was back on its hook. Again realisation dawned. This must be none other than the lantern he had seen in the cavern. His father must have taken it to the cove one night when he was helping Lobster Len and the others to land smuggled goods.

"If it *is* the same lantern that means Dad must have gone to the cove after I went to bed last night and brought it back with him," Michael said, but it distressed him to harbour such suspicions and he tried hard to think of some other explanation.

"Maybe Dad lent the lantern to someone," he told Nellie. "Come to that there may still be one in the cave. That will prove how wrong I am, and I'll be *glad*."

At least here was something Michael could do. He could set his mind at rest by going to the little cove to find out. But even as Michael shut the shed door an unusual sound made him stop to listen. Horse hooves were clattering down the cobbled street towards the cottage. Mum heard them too.

"Whoever can be riding at this time of day?" she asked, but Michael was already running round the front to find out.

CHAPTER FIVE

FROM BAD TO WORSE

"Hello Mike! You didn't think you'd be seeing me today, did you?" the rider called and Michael was delighted to see that it was Trevor who drew the pony to a halt.

"Or me," added Beth, who was sitting behind her brother.

She wore a new blue riding cloak with a fur-lined hood and looked very snug and warm.

"No, this certainly is a surprise. What brought you all this way and so early too?"

"It was Mum," Trevor explained. "She's got a lot of baking to do this morning and later on today there's going to be some sort of committee meeting in our house. The wine merchant next door and some other merchants are coming. That's why Mum wants us out of the way."

"I know what it's all about," Beth said in a loud whisper. "It's about all the tea and brandy that's being sold free of duty and . . ."

"Ssssh!" Michael exclaimed.

"But it is, I heard Daddy say . . ."

"Beth, for the last time will you stop repeating things you overhear," Trevor said sharply. "You're becoming a proper Priscilla Pry and it's not nice."

He twisted round in his saddle and glared angrily at his sister.

"Why don't you dismount?" Michael asked. "It's ages since Mum saw you. She'll be ever so pleased you've come."

At that moment Mrs. Trevane came out of the cottage to welcome Trevor and Beth.

"You must be thirsty after your ride. Come in and have some hot milk," she said.

As Trevor and Beth jumped down beside him it seemed to Michael that a load of worries rolled off his back. Things did not seem half as black now that he had his cousins to talk to. He felt almost lighthearted as he led the way round the back and helped Trevor give the pony a quick rub down.

"There's room for him in the shed beside Nellie, he'll be company for her," Michael said.

Meanwhile Beth was already making herself at home in the Trevanes' cottage.

"It was lovely riding over the Goonhilly Downs. I like the cold air on my face," she said. "I wanted to ride all day in my new riding hood but Trevor wouldn't let me. Do you like it, Auntie?"

"It's smart all right. What a lucky girl you are," Mrs. Trevane replied. "Your uncle's asleep because he was out late last night, but you must show it to him later. Here's your milk, drink it while it's hot."

"Let's do something out of the ordinary today," Trevor said, as he, too, sipped a mug of hot milk.

"Yes let's. Nothing different ever happens in our dull town. It's much nicer when you've got the sea and cliffs, and rocks to climb," Beth said.

"They're all pretty ordinary to me, you know," Michael grinned. "It doesn't matter though. You say what you want to do."

"I'd like to explore the beach," Trevor said.

"All right then, the sea's been jolly rough lately and could have washed up something worth finding," Michael agreed. "It's best when there's been a wreck out on the rocks, all sorts of things get washed up. We feel sorry for the sailors of course, but once I found a pistol that worked and a knife with ever such a sharp blade. I also found a telescope. . . ."

"What fun! Hasn't there been a wreck lately?" Beth asked.

"Don't be so hopeful! You forget people get drowned in shipwrecks," Trevor said.

"Last winter there were three wrecks on the Devil's Teeth alone. It was awful really," Michael said quietly. "I'm glad we've had none this winter."

"I think the sea's grand, yet it can be so cruel," Trevor agreed.

"You're always telling me off, yet you know I wouldn't want anyone to come to harm," Beth said with a pout.

"Come on, the tide's going out this morning so we'll be able to get a good way round the rocks," Michael said.

He was glad Trevor had suggested going to the beach. It would make it easy for him to slip into the cavern and see if there was still a lantern on the ledge.

"I'll show you my favourite cave if you like," Michael offered and Trevor was thrilled.

"Can you go a long way inside it?" he asked.

"I'd keep to the beach if I were you. You don't want to get cold in damp caves," Mrs. Trevane said nervously. "And what about taking Nellie to the cliff top? Your father won't want her today and she needs exercise. She should find something to eat up there too."

"All right, I'll take her," Michael agreed.

"Can I ride her bare-backed?" Beth asked, still anxious to show off her new riding hood.

"If she'll let you, but don't blame me if she tips you off," Michael replied.

Trevor was eager to be off and ran on ahead up the narrow track to the cliff top. But he soon became out of breath and had to slow down.

"It's queer going up to get to the beach," he panted.

"We've had to come this way because of Nellie, and anyway I want to show you my secret path into a little cove," Michael said. "You can get to the cove by climbing over masses of fallen rock, but it's more fun this way."

Michael left Nellie munching happily at some dried thistles on the cliff top and led the way down to the cove.

"I wish we had secret tracks and caves and things near us," Trevor said enviously.

"You can't expect to have caves in towns, silly," Michael replied. "You need the sea to wear the cliffs into hollows."

"Daddy thinks it's a shame you live here with hardly any friends just because of that old quarry," Beth said, turning to smile at Michael.

"I don't mind, I like the wildness. I couldn't live in a town," he replied. "Look, there's my favourite cave. Who's coming in?"

"Not me, it looks too dark and gloomy," Beth said.

"I'm going, you wait for us on the beach," Trevor said. "You can collect shells, you found some good ones last time we were here, remember?"

"Don't be long," Beth replied, pouncing on an unbroken oyster shell.

"I'll go first," Michael said. "This cave opens out into a big cavern and there's a bit of light once you get there."

They felt their way along the cave with only the slippery wall to guide them until they reached the cavern. Michael peered about him in the dim light. Suddenly he gasped with astonishment.

"Trevor! Just look at these kegs and oilskin bags," he exclaimed.

"Oh ho, and who said no smuggling went on here?" Trevor shouted accusingly. "I bet I know what's in those oilskin bags. Tea! Smugglers always use those sort of bags."

He ran forward and felt one. "It's tea all right," he said, slapping the offending bag. "The smuggled tea that's turning my Dad into a poor man! I'm going to rip those bags and dump the beastly stuff into the sea! Look at those kegs as well. Full of brandy or rum they are, no wonder our neighbour's having a tough time too. If this goes on everyone will starve who doesn't handle contraband."

But Michael scarcely heard Trevor's angry outburst. The discovery had all but stunned him.

"Come on, Mike, help me dump this tea in the sea," Trevor shouted.

He grabbed one of the bags but it weighed nearly

thirty pounds and he could hardly lift it.

"Don't be crazy! We could never shift that lot," Michael objected. "Anyway, Trev, we mustn't touch it, honestly we mustn't. Let's go."

But Trevor would not listen. He searched the cavern until he came to the ledge where the lantern had been. Michael watched him uneasily and his stomach gave a lurch when he saw that the lantern had gone. Near to the ledge Trevor found a narrow cleft in the rock. He put his hand in and pulled out a small leather bag.

"Look at these, Mike. Coins," he said, holding out two in the palm of his hand. Even in the half light Michael was sure they were the same as the one he had found at home.

"It's hard to tell what they are in this light," Trevor said excitedly, "but they are either Portuguese moidores or Spanish pistoles."

"Put them back, all this is nothing to do with us," Michael protested, and turned to leave the cavern.

"Nothing to do with us isn't it?" Trevor stormed. "Don't you care that smuggling's ruining my Dad's trade? I tell you people won't buy his goods when they can get them for half the price from smugglers. Don't you understand? This cave is full of contraband!"

"I understand only too well," Michael replied, "and there's something important I've got to tell you. Not in here though, let's go back to the beach."

Trevor did not miss the note of urgency in his cousin's voice and followed him quietly into the daylight. Beth was so busy searching for shells that she did not notice them come out, and Michael was glad.

"Quick, let's slip up the cliff path and hide," he whispered.

They crouched down behind a large rock and Michael poured out the whole story, beginning with the men in the quarry and ending with the gold coin he had found.

"At first I thought the men were pinching Dad's granite, but Mum was so upset when I told her that I couldn't help suspecting there must be some connection between what I'd seen and Lobster Len coming to our house."

"There's a connection right enough," Trevor said grimly. "It's as plain as day that your Dad's helping smugglers. Lobster Len and his gang do the risky part running the cargoes ashore and taking them up to the quarry. After that the men they're in league with whisk everything across the Downs and sell it."

"Whatever's come over Dad to let them use his quarry?" Michael said, more to himself than to Trevor.

"You bet they make it worth his while," Trevor said in disgust.

"I wouldn't have told all this to anyone in the world but you," Michael went on. "What can I do, Trev? I can't sneak on my own Dad, can I? I hope you won't go off me now you know the truth."

"Of course I won't go off you. We're all in this mess together and you and I have got to find a way out, that's all."

Trevor whistled softly to himself and looked deep in thought. Michael cupped his chin in his hands and tried to sort things out too. It was he who at last broke the silence between them.

"I wish my Dad hadn't given up going to church," he sighed. "He's only got mixed up with smugglers because he's forgotten about God and what the Bible says."

"Mr. Wesley was only talking about that yesterday evening," Trevor said in surprise. "He said we soon forget what the Bible teaches if we don't hear it read regularly. Then we easily fall when the devil tempts us. The trouble with the devil is, he knows how to make wrong things look so nice, doesn't he?"

"Yes, and yet it's never too late to turn back to God. That's what Mr. Wesley said in the market place and . . . and I was glad it wasn't too late for me," Michael said hesitantly.

"It wouldn't be too late for your Dad either, if only we could get him out of the grip of these smugglers. Get him out we must, Mike! Do you know you can be put in prison for smuggling? I've even heard of some smugglers who were transported to America. They died there and never saw their wives and children again."

Michael shuddered. "The trouble is it's so much nicer for Dad to have more money," he said. "We have lots to eat nowadays and he's even talked of getting another pony soon. Blow the devil for the way he tempts!"

"As you get richer, so we get poorer," Trevor said, with a wry smile.

"I don't care a hang about the money. I'd rather be poor and happy and . . . and have all of us honest,"

Michael replied.

"I wonder if it would help if you told your Dad all you know. Do you think it would upset him enough to make him want to stop?" Trevor asked.

"I'm not so sure about that. It might make him hopping mad," Michael said despondently. "And don't forget now that the smugglers have got him in their grip they might not easily let him go."

And there was more truth in that statement than even Michael could have guessed.

CHAPTER SIX

LOBSTER LEN

"Yooee! Trev, Mike, where are you?"

"We'll have to go or Beth will wonder what's happened to us," Trevor said, rubbing the pins and needles from his cramped legs. "It's a thing knowing what to do for the best, isn't it?"

"I wish you didn't live so far away, it makes it hard to keep in touch," Michael replied, "but we'll have to do it and . . . and both think hard of some way to help."

"We must pray, that's the main thing," Trevor said. "Don't forget God's always there ready to hear us, it's only us that forget to keep in touch with Him."

"Trevor, where are you?"

"Coming," he shouted and Michael slid after him down the narrow path.

"Where've you been?" Beth demanded. "I've shouted my head off at the cave entrance. "Did you come out another way?"

"No. I say what a lovely stone you've got there," Trevor said. "It glinted purple as you held it up."

"Mauve I'd call it. Actually it's a piece of amethyst," Michael said. "Rich ladies wear brooches and rings made from it."

"Goodness, I wouldn't fancy a bit of that on my finger," Beth said.

"Silly you! It would be very different from that

after a craftsman had shaped and polished it,"
Michael grinned. "The amethyst inside the stone
would shine like coloured glass. I've found several
precious stones on this beach. Crystal is fairly common
but sometimes I find rose quartz, which is a lovely
pink colour, but it's hard to find."

"Fancy knowing the names of so many different
stones. You are clever," Beth said.

"It's my Dad who's clever, not me. What he doesn't
know about stones, precious or otherwise, isn't worth
knowing," Michael told her.

"This isn't the beach we came on last time is it?"
Trevor asked. "Where's the beach with the fishing
boats and lobster pots?"

"Beyond all that fallen rock. Would you like to go
there?" Michael suggested.

"Yes, please, it's ages since I've seen a boat," Beth
said. "I'd like to go out in one."

"You can't go in a boat dressed in your riding cloak,
it would soon get messed up," Trevor said. "You'd
need an oilskin and sou'wester."

"Come on, we can look at the boats anyway,"
Michael said, and he led the way across the massive
boulders. He jumped from rock to rock nimble as a
goat, and was soon way ahead of the others.

"Hey, wait for us," Beth called, and she was so bad
at clambering over the rough rocks that Michael had
to go back and help her.

At last they came to the main beach and Michael
was relieved to be away from the small cove with its
secret of smuggled cargo.

"I've never noticed that before," Trevor said. He

pointed to where the cliff sloped gently to the beach. There Trevor could see the ruins of a tiny stone building, the remains of which were on a level with the beach.

"You'll never guess what that was, and there's not much left to tell you," Michael said.

Beth ran to the ruin and walked all round the tiny foundation area.

"It was a little house," she said.

"Not a house, but a chapel," Michael told her. "Grandpa once said that when he was a boy parts of the wall still stood but the sea gradually knocked them down."

"What a silly place to build a chapel," Trevor said.

"Yes, it didn't have a chance on the edge of the beach like that," Michael agreed. "If only it had been built further back we might still be having services in it. I wish we had a chapel in the village."

"Yes, it would serve to remind folks what's right and what isn't," Trevor said meaningly.

Michael gave him a warning frown but Beth, for once, was not listening.

"Look, Trev," she exclaimed. "You see that man coming towards us? I've seen him before. He was in the market the other day talking to Rock Rufus."

Michael turned to see who was coming. "Oh crumbs, it's Lobster Len," he muttered.

"Do you know him?" Beth asked.

"Of course. I know everyone in the village. What did you say about Rock Rufus? Isn't he the man who stopped John Wesley preaching yesterday?"

"That's right, he's a great bully and this man looks

48

like one too."

"Ssssh!" Michael said, for Lobster Len was coming uncomfortably near.

"Here, what are you kids doing on the beach?" he shouted.

"Looking at the chapel ruins," Michael replied.

"Oh, so it's you, is it?" Lobster Len said, his voice dropping to an unusually low and wheedling tone. He even managed to smile, and Michael thought it particularly unpleasant of him.

"Taking your friends sightseeing, are you?" Lobster Len went on. "Where else have you been?"

"We wanted to see a fishing boat," Michael replied evasively. "Can we look at yours?"

For a moment Lobster Len was off his guard. His eyes narrowed and he looked at Michael suspiciously. Michael returned his look unflinchingly and Lobster Len half-smiled again.

"Not today, my dears," he said. "Just taking her out to set a few lobster pots, I am. And anyway, you youngsters want to watch it, the tide's coming in. Not safe for strangers, this beach isn't. Not when the tide's coming in."

"The tide's going out right now," Michael said calmly, and Beth began to giggle.

"Fancy a fisherman not knowing that," she tittered and immediately Lobster Len flew into a rage.

"Get off my beach, you saucy young bit," he bawled. "Get off and stay off, d'you hear me? If I catch you hanging round again you'll find out more to the sea than whether it's ebbing or flowing! Clear off, and quick!"

Michael wanted to withstand Lobster Len and remind him that it was not *his* beach, but common sense warned him it was better not to argue. The sooner they went the better, before Lobster Len asked any more awkward questions.

"Goodbye little chapel. I hope someone will rebuild you one day," Beth said as she slowly moved away, and Michael was surprised that she showed so little fear of Lobster Len.

"But then she doesn't know as much about him as I do," he thought.

Trevor, on the contrary, was quite shaken by the encounter.

"Beth, are you sure you know that man? I mean, did you really see him talking to Rock Rufus?" he asked.

"Yes, it was him all right, and they went off to the tavern together. They looked good friends, Rock Rufus had his arm round Lobster Len's shoulders."

Michael and Trevor found it hard to hide their dismay.

"You two look ever so worried. What does it matter?" Beth asked, her eyes alight with curiosity.

Michael mumbled something about it being unusual for a fisherman to leave the sea and go inland to find friends, and that only made Beth more curious than ever.

"What can have made them so friendly?" she asked.

"Prissy Pry, one of these days you'll be in trouble for being so nosey," Trevor said sharply.

"How you love telling me off," Beth said, then away she skipped.

"I don't think much of Lobster Len's way of taking his lobster pots out," Trevor whispered to Michael. "He hasn't been near his boat. As soon as we moved off he clambered over the rocks the way we had come. I watched him out of the corner of my eye."

"I guessed as much. Just because Dad works the quarry Lobster Len thinks I know nothing about fishing, but that's where he's wrong. For a start I know jolly well that you only put lobster pots down in the summer, and here we are in the middle of winter. And fancy trying to tell us the tide was coming in! He was blustering all right. You bet he knows more about that hidden tea than we do. Honestly Trev, whatever came over my Dad to get mixed up with a rotter like that? And what can you do to stop it?"

"For the moment only pray, and I shouldn't say 'only' because praying's a big thing to do. God can guide us better than anyone."

Michael sighed and wished his faith was as deep and as strong as Trevor's. He was sure he ought to do something else as well as pray, but what could a boy like him do to outwit a gang of smugglers?

CHAPTER SEVEN

THE MOONSHINERS

Before Trevor and Beth went home they invited Michael to spend a day with them.

"And make it soon. Mummy was cross with you for not coming in yesterday," Beth said.

"It was only because I had to be back before dark," Michael replied.

"Can Mike have a whole day with us next week?" Trevor asked Mrs. Trevane, and she readily gave permission.

They decided on Tuesday, and none of them had the slightest foreboding of what an eventful day it would be.

Michael watched his cousins mount their pony and waved until they were out of sight. Then he set about cleaning out Nellie's shed, chopping up driftwood and sweeping out the back yard.

"Where's Nellie?" asked his mother, from the back door.

"Still on the cliff top, I'll fetch her when I've finished."

"Why didn't you bring her back with you this morning?"

"Because we didn't come that way. We climbed over the rocks to the main beach and I showed Trev and Beth where our little chapel used to be. I wish it hadn't fallen down. It was stupid to build it on the edge of the sand," Michael said.

"Perhaps it will be rebuilt one day. I've heard it talked about from time to time but that's as far as it's got as yet," Mrs. Trevane said. "Hurry up and fetch Nellie. Your father will be hungry when he comes in and supper will soon be ready."

But Michael did not feel like hurrying. When he reached the cliff top he saw Nellie poking about among some dry furze bushes. He called her to him then went to the edge of the cliff and sat down. It was so quiet up there, with only the occasional cry of a seabird and the sound of the waves slapping the rocks down below.

"What a difference it makes when the sun's shining and there's no wind," Michael said, caressing Nellie's silky nose. "The sea looks so calm and friendly today. Even the Devil's Teeth don't look as if they could do much harm."

Although he did not say it aloud, Michael wished that his own life was as calm and untroubled as the sea before him. He felt he was fighting an invisible wave of evil that threatened to make shipwreck of his life. Supposing the Revenue men caught his father helping smugglers? Supposing he was tried at the Assizes and transported to America? Supposing Lobster Len turned nasty? Supposing . . . and it seemed to Michael that the way ahead was overcast with cloudfuls of trouble and danger.

Suddenly a vessel out to sea attracted his attention. He shaded his eyes and watched her come nearer.

"I thought as much, it's the Revenue cutter from Penzance," Michael told Nellie. She looked a graceful sight with her sails billowing in the light breeze. She was swift too and Michael knew that any ship carrying contraband would be hard put to it once that Revenue cutter gave chase. But, of course, Revenue cutters, and the officers who sailed them, could only be in one place at a time.

"Too much smuggling goes on where the Customs men aren't looking," Michael said, flinging his arms out in a gesture of despair.

Yet he knew full well that if any Revenue men asked questions in his village, he would be among the first to put them off the scent.

"What else *could* I do?" he said, slapping Nellie on the flank. "Come on, we'd better go home."

That night Michael could not sleep. He tried praying but it did not calm him as it had done before. He tried to tell himself that God would make everything come right in the end.

"Yet how can He if Dad won't stop helping those smugglers?"

Before he found an answer to that question Michael heard a door open and shut.

"That was the back door, someone's gone out . . . or come in," Michael said, and in one bound he was out of bed. He crept half-way down the ladder and listened but all was quiet and the cottage was in darkness. He came right down and tip-toed to the back room to look out of the window. In the yard Michael saw someone light the lantern and open the door of Nellie's shed. He also saw Nellie's shadowy form being led out and watched his father take her round the side of the cottage.

Michael wanted to shout "Stop! Stop! Don't do it, Dad! Don't go wherever you're going," but the lump in his throat would not let him shout, even if it had been a wise thing to do. He ran to the front room and peered out. The lantern was dimmed, but its faint glow was enough to tell Michael which way his father was going—towards the path that led up the cliff.

Sleep was out of the question for Michael. He climbed back to the loft, dressed hurriedly, then returned to the front room.

"We can't go on like this. I'll have to tell Dad everything I know, like Trevor said," he muttered.

He sat on a stool by the window and watched and waited. At last Michael heard the sound of muffled footsteps. With the help of fitful moonlight he watched twenty or more fishermen go by. They walked warily, each man with his head bent low. All were heavily laden with a tea bag or keg on either shoulder.

"Wretched moonshiners!" Michael said between clenched teeth.

Last of all he saw Mr. Trevane leading Nellie and she was the most laden of all. She, too, walked with her head down as if she were ashamed of the heavy kegs she carried.

Not a word was spoken as the men passed and to Michael it was the grimmest, most sinister scene he had ever witnessed. It made the crime seem even worse now that he had actually seen the smugglers carrying their unlawful loads. Michael knew they were bound for the quarry, but he had no desire to follow them. It was bad enough meeting Lobster Len

in broad daylight. To catch him redhanded by moonlight would be asking for trouble.

So Michael stayed indoors and continued to wait.
He was prepared to wait until daybreak if necessary.
And the only thing that comforted him at all was that
his mother was apparently fast asleep and did not
know what was going on.

It seemed a long time before Michael heard the
clip-clop of Nellie's hooves on the cobbles. He went to
the back of the cottage and poked up the dying embers
in the range. He was still coaxing the fire to life when
his father came in.

"Why, lad, what are you doing up?" he asked.

"Waiting for you," Michael said, and his mouth
suddenly went dry. He looked appealingly at his
father.

"I've got to tell you something, Dad," he said.
"Don't think I've been deliberately spying because I
haven't, but I know you're helping smugglers. Mum's
upset about it and so am I. We can manage without
the extra money, honestly, Dad . . ."

Michael paused to lick his lips and his father sank
into a chair.

"So you know," his father said, passing his hand
wearily across his brow. "You mustn't think badly of
me, lad. It was only poverty that drove me to it. I
couldn't bear to see you so ill clad and your mother in
rags . . . and all of us hungry."

Michael knelt in front of his father and all at once
it seemed that a barrier between them had gone.
Almost without realising it, Michael knew that he had
been avoiding his father. He had not wanted to talk to

him or have meals with him. Now it was over and they were looking at their problem together.

"Mum and I don't mind being poor and hungry, Dad, but we would mind if you were caught and thrown in prison or . . . or exported."

"*Exported?* You make me sound like a bale of wool," said his father, trying to smile.

"Well it does happen," Michael replied.

"Listen, lad, there are many things you don't understand," his father said, and there was no anger in his voice. "For one thing, when I first agreed to let Lobster Len and his pals store a few kegs in the quarry there seemed nothing to it. In fact I was glad he was showing friendly at last. But you see things have a way of growing and now so much stuff is dumped there that I'm hard put to it to hide it from my workmen."

"Dad!"

"I was a fool, I should have remembered that wrong has a way of growing. It's like harmless baby sharks that grow until they're big enough to eat you."

Michael grimaced. "You said I wouldn't understand, but I do."

"I haven't finished yet," his father said. "You're upset that smuggling goes on here, but there's another side to it. Smuggling's become a way of life to lots of folk recently. It's not what they want, but they would starve otherwise. And here's something else you won't have thought of. The tax on tea, salt and spirits is ruinous. It's a scandal the heights to which taxation has soared. Reduce the duty on imported goods, give the poor man a chance to earn an honest living, and 'moonshining' would die a natural death."

Michael frowned. "You're right, Dad. I can't understand all that about taxes," he said. "But I do know Uncle Arthur's business is being ruined by free trading. People won't buy his tea when they can get it half the price from smugglers. He's becoming poorer every day. I know because Trevor told me."

And now it was Mr. Trevane's turn to be dismayed.

"My own brother! Oh, why haven't I thought of him before?"

Michael said nothing. The issues at stake were more complicated than he had realised. He only knew that one simple fact remained. Smuggling was wrong. You could be imprisoned for it. You could even be hanged for it. And *his* father was in league with smugglers.

"Don't look so worried, lad," his father said. "Lobster Len is not the leader of the gang. He's in the pay of a much bigger shark . . ."

"Yes, Rock Rufus."

"Mike, what don't you know?"

"Beth pointed him out to me. He tried to stop Mr. Wesley preaching the other day. She told me he was a moonshiner."

"Yes, but he's not satisfied with present arrangements. He doesn't like his cargoes being carried across the Downs to Helston. A rival gang's using the Helford River at present, but when they've come to terms he won't need our help any more."

Mr. Trevane could have added that Lobster Len had threatened to expose Rock Rufus to Excise Officers if he took his 'trade' away, but the less said about that the better for Michael's peace of mind.

"I'll tell you something else," Mr. Trevane went on. "Rumours are abroad that the whole matter of duty and taxation is being gone into by Parliament in London. Once they've sorted it out everything will be all right anyway."

Michael sighed. How confusing it all was!

"But what about *now*, Dad? Can't you stop helping those smugglers?"

His father could not bear the distress in Michael's eyes. He turned away and gazed at the fire instead.

"Arthur, what am I doing to you?" he whispered, so softly that Michael only just heard his words. Michael left the room and flung himself on his bed in the loft.

"What's the use of talking? What's the use of praying? Why can't I *do* something?" he said, pummelling the straw mattress with clenched fists.

CHAPTER EIGHT

MORE OF THE MOONSHINERS

Michael knew that the barrier between him and his father was up again. Neither said any more about smuggling, in fact they did not speak much at all. Michael hated feeling so cut off, and it did nothing to solve the problem of how to rid the village of smuggling.

Altogether Michael had never felt so isolated in his life. He knew his mother would be very distressed if he told her what he had seen, and he shrank from upsetting her. But one thing Michael was determined about. He *would* stop those moonshiners, no matter how long it took him to hit on a plan.

At last it was Tuesday and Michael cheered up at the thought of seeing Trevor again. He had already decided to tell him everything and maybe between them they would think of a way to outwit the smugglers.

"We'll have to do it before the Revenue Officers pounce and lock them all up," Michael said as he set off astride Nellie's back.

A strong wind swept up the narrow village street and blew dust from the quarry into Michael's face. He shut his eyes and urged Nellie on until they reached the Goonhilly Downs. There the wind raged at full gale force, howling and whistling across the scrub. It tugged at Michael's hair and he shivered as he pulled his cloak more closely round him.

"Crumbs! I'd be as bald as a boulder if this gale had its way," he shouted to Nellie, but the wind snatched his words away.

It was the roughest ride Michael had ever had astride the faithful little donkey. Several times he had to crouch low to stop himself from being blown off her back. Part of the way he was forced to dismount and walk beside her, but Michael was determined that nothing would prevent him from going to Helston.

After a while he passed a tumbledown moorhouse that had once been the refuge of tinners. No one laboured for tin in those parts now, and Michael's Grandpa had told him that life was grim for tinners even when he was a boy. The moorhouse consisted of one windowless room and its only comfort was a wide hearth for burning furze and turf. The tinners used to sleep on dried heather and ate rabbits, woodcock, duck and any other creatures they could trap in the marshes or scrubland.

"Fancy spending a winter up here slogging for tin!" Michael said. And the moorhouse looked so lonely and dejected that it was plainly a long time since any tinners had thought it worth the struggle.

The old moorhouse was the only sign of habitation until at last Michael reached Helston. Although it was not market day the town was crowded with people hurrying to and fro. Michael wondered what they were doing and where they were going. He crossed the market place and went on to the better part of the town where his cousins lived.

"Look at you! Your hair's standing on end," Beth

squealed, running out to meet him.

"So would yours be if you'd battled against the wind on the Downs," Michael grinned.

Beth prattled on but Michael hardly listened. His one wish was to get Trevor on his own and tell him about the smuggling he had watched. His chance came after dinner when an elderly gentleman came to give Beth a singing lesson.

"Let's go out," Trevor said, and Michael agreed readily. He told his story as they walked towards the market place and finished it as they sat down on the steps to the market house.

"It's all so complicated," Michael concluded. "When Dad came home he told me people have got to smuggle because of the high tax on salt and things. We must have salt in our village because of the pilchards that are preserved in it, but the fishermen can't afford the tax on it so they smuggle it ashore."

"But that's not the whole story. What about the tea and rum that are hidden in your Dad's quarry, putting honest men like my Dad out of business. It's up to . . ."

Trevor broke off at the sound of a loud, coarse laugh behind him. A moment later Rock Rufus lumbered down the market house steps followed by someone else. Michael recognised the second man at once. It was Lobster Len.

"I knew it was Lobster Len even before I saw him," Michael whispered. "I'd know his laugh anywhere. Come on, let's follow and see where they're going."

"Rather!" Trevor agreed, his voice shrill with excitement.

"If only we could find out where they hide their

stuff here," Michael went on. "We could get your Dad to tell the Revenue Officer or the magistrate and Rock Rufus would be caught redhanded. . . . The only thing is I don't want my Dad dragged into it."

"He wouldn't be if we can find their store here. Ssssh, don't let them see or hear us," Trevor whispered.

They followed the smugglers until they came to a tavern, and watched them go inside.

"We can't go in, Lobster Len would recognise me at once," Michael said.

"Pity Beth wasn't with us. She would have overheard what they were saying on the way," Trevor replied.

They went as near to the door as they dared but could only hear shouting and laughter within.

"Sounds like the whole gang in there, they might stay for ages," Michael said, his voice full of disappointment.

"Just when we were on to something!" Trevor exclaimed, as they slipped into a nearby doorway.

While they were wondering what to do next the tavern door crashed open and Rock Rufus lunged into the street. This time two men followed him, the newcomer being small and weedy with a face like a weasel. Michael and Trevor watched them turn into a narrow side street and lost no time in following.

"They look pretty grim and determined, I'd like to know what plans they're hatching," Michael whispered.

"Ssssh!" Trevor cautioned.

The men turned a corner into another, dingier

street and Michael and Trevor were just in time to see them disappear into a narrow passage between two shabby houses. As the cousins crept nearer they could hear the men arguing.

"I still think it's risky staging another one on the same coast so soon," piped up the weasel-like man in a nervous, high-pitched voice.

"Aw, shut-up Wippet. You've only got to cross the Downs to see what the wind's like. Folk expect ship-wrecks this weather..." came the voice of Lobster Len.

"Quit squabbling," Rock Rufus growled. "We've work to do. How can I plan things with you two scrapping? As for you, Wippet, you can't funk it now. You're in with us up to the neck. Any more squealing and I'll deal with you private like."

"I'm not squealing, I've got a house laid on for the job, haven't I? Went to a lot of trouble finding some-where suitable if you want to know."

"Are we going to see the place or aren't we?" Lobster Len asked.

Michael and Trevor waited until the men's foot-steps died away then ran silently up the arched pas-sage towards another, wider street. They peered out cautiously and saw Rock Rufus and his companions climb the front steps of an old house on the far side of the road. It was the sort of house a merchant would have once lived in with a trap door in the pavement for goods to be lowered into the cellar.

Michael watched the man called Wippet stumble over the doorstep and saw Rock Rufus drag him into the house by the scruff of the neck. He also saw

Lobster Len kick the unfortunate man from behind
to help him on his way.

"Nice lot!" Trevor whispered, "but the thing is
what did they mean about shipwrecks? It sounded
pretty shady to me."

"It was shady all right," Michael said. "Surely
you've heard of wreckers, Trev? They shine false
lights and make boats founder on the rocks. Last winter a big boat broke up on the Devil's Teeth and
several Revenue men came to our village and made a
fuss about it. Everyone on the boat was drowned and
the Customs Officers suspected the boat had been
lured in on purpose, specially as all the cargo had
gone before they arrived. Nothing was proved but
from what we've just heard it sounds as if the Revenue
men were right and Rock Rufus is being wicked
enough to plan another wreck!"

Michael trembled as he spoke and his face was
drawn and drained of all colour.

"This is something too big for us. We can't cope,"
Trevor whispered and he too was clearly shaken.
"We'd better go, there's nothing we can do except
tell. . . ."

"Nothing we can do!" Michael cut in. "Isn't this
just the chance we've been waiting for? I'm going to
find out more of their plans if it's the last thing I do."

"You can't, Mike. Don't be crazy!"

"If I'm crazy it's only because I've a chance to do
something at last," Michael said. "Look, the wind's
blown the door ajar . . . those idiots didn't shut it
properly. Luck's on my side for once. I'm going into
that house. If you're scared, wait here."

Trevor could see Michael had made up his mind and did not argue further.

"I reckon I'd better wait here," he said. "The thing is there's no point in us both being caught spying. But do be careful, Mike. They could kill you."

"They won't get the chance," Michael replied through clenched teeth. He peered up and down the dingy street and saw that it was quite deserted. Then he took another look at the house opposite. To his relief all the windows were shuttered. At least he could cross the road without being spotted from within.

CHAPTER NINE

A SHOCK FOR MICHAEL

Michael took a deep breath, then darted across the street and up the broken steps. The door creaked faintly as he pushed it further open and slipped inside. He found himself in a dark, musty hall and the sound of voices told him that Rock Rufus and the others had gone into a room at the back of the house. Michael took off his shoes and tip-toed along the hall until he was near enough to hear what they were saying.

"What news of the ship?" he heard Rock Rufus ask.

"She's a Spanish vessel bound for Plymouth. Laden with silks and laces she is, and a nice drop of Spanish wine to wash the sea taste from our mouths when we've finished with her," said Lobster Len.

"Just a small matter of making the cargo ours," Rock Rufus replied.

"She's still battling with the wind, but rest on it she'll want shelter for the night. She'll never make the Lizard in this gale," Lobster Len assured him.

"Couldn't be better. You've done well to find out that much."

"I even know the ship's name. She's the 'Señorita Maria'," Lobster Len boasted.

"I'd like to know how you find out so much," the Wippet said plaintively.

"You stick to your job and I'll stick to mine," Lobster Len said.

"I was banking on tonight, my friends," Rock Rufus went on. "By all accounts she's a big ship with a full cargo to clear before dawn. I've sounded my tinner contacts in Germoe and they're more than willing to give us a hand. Their leader should have turned up at the tavern by now ready for the final word from me. I'll suggest we meet up with them at the old moorhouse. They're bringing a couple of carts with them. Mind you, we'll have to watch it or they'll pinch more than their share of the takings."

"We'd better push off as soon as we've looked at the cellars," Lobster Len said, "and when I get back I'll rustle up the local chaps. You'll find us in the cove, not the main beach."

"We only want the toughest types," Rock Rufus reminded him. "No good getting youngsters who turn squeamish at the sight of a body or two washed up with the tide."

"Ugh! The cargo's all right, but the thought of men drowning to give it to us. . . ."

"Aw shut-up, Windy Wippet. Another squeal from you and you'll taste the leather of my belt," Rock Rufus threatened.

"I'll be on duty here and have a house warming ready for you and the cargo—hatch oiled, candles in the cellar, the lot," the Wippet said in wheedling tones.

"You'll do nothing of the sort, you're coming with us," Rock Rufus replied. "Your job will be to shine the lantern from the cliff top."

"T . . . th . . . the lantern? You mean the l . . . light to lure the 'Señorita Maria' onto the D . . . Devil's Teeth?" the Wippet asked, and Michael could almost hear his teeth chattering as he spoke. Then the wretched man became quite hysterical, his voice rising to a shrill squeak.

"I've done my bit, guv. I found this place to hide the stuff. I bribed the Clerk too and . . ."

"Either you shine that lantern or down in the cellar you go, bound hand and foot until we get back. You double-crossing ferret, what's your game, eh? Not coming, aren't you? Crying off, are you? We risk our necks to fill your pockets with gold pistoles worth eighteen shillings a piece do we?" Rock Rufus snarled. "Or would you be sneaking on us for a fat reward?"

Michael heard a scuffle and a cry, then Lobster Len spoke up.

"Forget him, guv. I know a much better bloke to shine the lantern for us. I mean Trevane, who lets us use his quarry."

Further scuffling followed, but Michael could not wait to see if the Wippet really was thrown into the cellar. He dare not risk discovery. Icy fear gripped his heart and he turned and fled from the house.

"Mike! Whatever's up? Have you seen a ghost?" Trevor asked.

"I can't tell you now. Come on!" Michael said, dragging on his shoes. He dashed through the narrow passage, along this street, down that and Trevor ran with him without any idea what it was about.

They ran until they were well past the tavern and

only stopped then because they were too puffed to run any further.

"Trev, I must get home quickly. Will you lend me your pony?" Michael panted. Trevor nodded, too out of breath to answer.

"Rock Rufus and his gang have turned wreckers. ... They want my Dad to shine a false light to-night. . . . It's a Spanish ship they're after. . . ."

Trevor had to be satisfied with this explanation as he led his pony from the stable.

"Don't bother about a saddle. I'll ride bare-back," Michael said.

In a second he was astride the pony and off, leaving his bewildered cousin standing in the yard. Nellie, too, was bewildered at being left behind and brayed her protest loudly.

"Sorry, Nell, you're too slow," Michael shouted over his shoulder. Never had he crossed the Downs at the speed he went that day. Trevor's pony must have sensed the urgency of his mission and galloped like the wind that had set his mane and tail a-flying.

"Dad can't do such a thing . . . I've got to warn him . . . got to get there first . . ."

On past great boulders that stood like sentinels defying the wind and storm, past the moorhouse, past heather and scrub. . . . How much further was it? Supposing Lobster Len had the start of him? Supposing he also had a swift pony and was already galloping some way ahead?

And then Michael became calmer. Of course Lobster Len could not have beaten him to it. What with tying the Wippet up and putting him in the cellar, then going to the tavern to see the tinner from Germoe, Lobster Len was probably only now starting out. He would not be in such a hurry anyway. It would be nightfall before he needed to get busy.

The pony slowed to a canter and then to a trot, but Michael urged him back to a canter. At last the track sloped downwards and they were nearly at the quarry. It was early afternoon and still light, so Michael knew he would find his father working there.

"Whether he'll be pleased to see me or not is another matter," Michael thought. "But this time he's got to listen. Deliberately wrecking a ship means murdering the whole crew!" and Michael shuddered as he thought of those rocky jaws where so many ships had broken their backs and so many seamen had found a watery grave.

The pony trotted to the quarry entrance and Michael jumped off.

"Thanks for the ride, you've been a real pal," Michael said, giving the pony a quick pat.

"If it's your father you want, he's over there," said the bent old man who chipped away at blocks of granite. He pointed a gnarled finger to the left and Michael saw his father working beside two of his men.

"Dad!"

Mr. Trevane turned and came towards him. "Yes, what is it, lad?" he asked, and Michael felt a twinge of pity at the strained look on his father's face. Clearly he was anything but a happy man.

"Come this way a bit, I've something important to

tell you," Michael said. They stood beside a large block of granite and Michael lost no time in pouring out his story. As he spoke his father's face became grimmer and grimmer.

"You wouldn't do such a thing, would you, Dad? Not for all the gold in the world, surely?" Michael ended breathlessly.

"I . . . How little I dreamed it would come to this," whispered his father, passing his hand across his brow. "How did you get here did you say?"

"On Trev's pony. I rode like the wind to warn you, so's you could be ready to refuse . . . and fight it out if necessary."

"I may need that pony, lad. Leave him here and go home to your mother, will you?"

"But, Dad . . ."

"Leave me, I've got to think this thing through."

Reluctantly Michael left the quarry and went home. As he walked round to the back of the cottage he suddenly remembered that he had left God out of everything that day and had not asked for His help.

"Oh, God, you know everything. You know the trouble we're in," he prayed in the small back yard. "Don't let the 'Señorita Maria' be lured onto the Devil's Teeth. Above all, dear God, please don't let Dad shine the false light that would bring her in . . . and forgive me for not believing like I should."

Then Michael hurried indoors to where Mrs. Trevane was. Whatever happened it was up to him to help her bear it. It was even up to him to do all he could to protect her from harm.

72

"Oh crumbs! I hope Mum won't ask where Nellie is," he muttered.

And he tried to think up a good excuse for leaving her with Trevor.

CHAPTER TEN

MICHAEL TO THE RESCUE

Michael whistled as he went indoors and grinned cheerfully. His mother had her arms deep in a wash tub and looked up in surprise to see Michael home so soon.

"Beth had a singing lesson and it was Trevor's turn after that," he said vaguely. "I say, Mum, it isn't half blowing a gale on the Downs. I should think we're in for a right old storm."

"Well, let's hope it won't take any more slates off the roof," replied his mother.

"If it does, I'll climb up and put them on again. How about that?"

Michael poured himself a mugful of milk and sat by the fire to drink it.

"Don't whistle, there's a good lad. It goes right through my head," Mrs. Trevane said. "Tell me what you did in Helston today."

"Not much ... well, you know, there wasn't any market or anything. The town seems ever so different when the market isn't full of stalls and people aren't shouting their heads off. Trev and I sat on the steps for a bit and could actually hear ourselves talk. On market days women in red and blue cloaks and big hats stand on those steps. They sell fish and just about yell their hats off at the posh ladies passing by."

"I can't imagine a posh lady walking off with a plaice or cod tucked under her arm," said his mother, laughing. "I suppose she would send her servant to buy one."

It was good to hear his mother laugh and Michael tried to recall other things that would amuse her as she worked. He told her of the fruit stall that he always saw on market days. It belonged to a funny little man who juggled with his apples in between serving customers.

"I've watched him juggling with as many as six at a time and he never drops one," Michael said. "The odd thing is he looks like an apple himself. He's round and dumpy and his face is as red as the apples he sells."

As Michael talked he kept wondering what his father was doing. Had Lobster Len spoken to him yet? Had his father refused to shine the fateful lantern? Could Lobster Len force him into it by threatening exposure if he didn't? If only his father had never agreed to store smuggled cargoes in his quarry! What a nightmare had grown from such small beginnings.

And then Michael thought of the baby sharks that one day grow big enough to eat you. He clearly remembered his father saying that in the same way little wrongs have a habit of growing so big that in the end you can't put them right.

"But it's never too late to turn to God. Never too late to ask Him to forgive you and help you to make a new start. . . ." Now it was John Wesley's words that Michael recalled. "Never too late! But it *could* be

75

too late for Dad if he agrees to shine that light and hangs for it!"

Michael shuddered and stared wide-eyed into the smouldering fire.

"You're quiet all of a sudden. Not chilled are you, lad? I'll make you that new cloak soon, you need it for those wild Downs," his mother said.

Michael nodded and gave the fire a poke.

"I'll bring some more wood from the shed when I've mangled these things," his mother went on.

"I'll get it," Michael said. "I'll mangle your washing too." He grabbed the basket of wet clothes and took it into the yard before his mother could thank him. Next he dived into the shed where Nellie slept and pulled out the mangle that Mrs. Trevane was so proud of. Apart from being the only one in the village, Uncle Arthur had had it specially made for her. It was very like the one used in his own household and Michael's mother thought the world of it.

"I don't mind turning that mangle, it makes me feel rich," she called.

"It should make you feel even richer to have a servant turning it for you," Michael called back gaily. If only he could have felt as gay as he sounded! Dusk was falling when Michael put the mangle away and took the washing indoors.

"I'll dry it round the fire tonight," said his mother. "We'd lose everything in this wind."

"Yes, you couldn't possibly hang it out," Michael agreed.

"Lay the table will you, lad? I expect your father will be in soon."

But time went by and still Michael's father did not come.

"What can have kept him?" Mrs. Trevane asked more than once. "It's pitch-dark now, he can't be working."

She became more and more agitated and inwardly Michael felt the same. He wondered uneasily whether his father had come to some agreement with Lobster Len. Then Michael remembered the pony. What did his father want him for? Where had he gone? Surely not to Helston with a gang of wreckers and the tinners from Germoe coming from the other direction. Rock Rufus would promptly turn him round and force him to come back with them.

"I've a feeling Dad's had an accident," Mrs. Trevane said suddenly. "What else could have kept him so late? A falling rock could have pinned him down and even now he may be lying with no one to help."

"But he's not alone at the quarry. He never tackles anything dangerous unless the men are around," Michael replied.

"Sometimes he doesn't see danger until it's too late," his mother said, and Michael could not have agreed with her more. "He might have called for help but the wind carried his cries away. Just listen to it! We're in for a storm all right."

Michael shuddered as he thought of the ship that would most definitely be in danger that night. Even now the 'Señorita Maria' would be fighting for her life as she rolled and plunged in the boiling sea, her sails in shreds.

77

"How she'll welcome that twinkling light beckoning her, so she'll think, to a harbour where she can safely anchor.... Oh, where *is* Dad? Can he have agreed to shine that light?"

"There's one other possibility, lad," his mother interrupted Michael's thoughts. "Dad could be helping some fishermen to land a ... a cargo."

Mrs. Trevane looked away as she said the word 'cargo' and Michael was strongly tempted to blurt out, "Why say 'fishermen' when you know you mean smugglers?" but he controlled himself.

"No one could land anything on a night like this," he said, forcing himself to speak calmly. "You could be right about the quarry though, Mum. I'll take the lantern and see if everything's all right."

"I don't like you going on your own, lad. If only our neighbours were more friendly someone could go with you. Why not ask? Most people will help when you are in real trouble."

"Don't worry, Mum, I know the way blindfold. I'll have a good look round and make sure Dad hasn't come to harm."

"Take Nellie with you for company."

"She's too slow in the dark, I can go quicker alone," Michael hedged. Then he grabbed his cloak and out he ran, tingling with excitement at the plan that had suddenly formed in his mind. He took the lantern from its hook and hurried into the street, but he did not go to the quarry. That would be wasting time. Michael knew that if his father was still at the quarry, Lobster Len and a whole gangful of wreckers would be there too and he, Michael, could do nothing about it.

"But if I go to the cliff top there is something I can do. I can save the 'Señorita Maria' and keep Dad out of trouble," Michael whispered. "How dense I am for not thinking of a way before!"

He did not dare to light the lantern but groped his way up the cliff path, hoping and praying that he was not too late. When Michael reached the cliff top he was horrified to find the wreckers had beaten him to it. Already the fateful lantern swung to and fro, its flame flickering a deadly welcome to the 'Señorita Maria' as she floundered in the inky sea.

Michael hesitated but a moment. He knew the cliff top well. He knew exactly where the heather grew thickest and the furze was driest. One thing he did not know was who was luring the 'Señorita Maria' to her doom.

"I don't care whether it's Dad or Rock Rufus himself. I'm saving that ship," Michael whispered. "Please, God, don't let me be too late!"

Michael crept along the cliff until he found the thick clump of furze that was a great favourite with Nellie. Next he pulled out his tinder box and lit the lantern, shielding the light with his cloak. He drew the lantern fully and the flame flared wildly.

"Right, I can't put that other light out, but I can make a brighter one. That ship will know this is a cliff top and no harbour when I've finished," Michael exclaimed.

Even as he spoke Michael flung his cloak aside and threw the lantern into the heather beneath the furze bush. His plan succeeded immediately. The heather burst into flames and the wind lifted the flames into the furze bush. Michael stared fascinated. Within seconds the whole bush was ablaze. The wind also carried sparks in all directions and small fires began wherever they landed, to be quickly fanned into a roaring blaze.

"Fire! Fire!" someone yelled, and Michael turned to see the man with the lantern running towards the cliff path.

"Bother, he's blocked my way of escape," Michael muttered.

"Fire!" the man yelled again, and even in the panic that gripped him, Michael was greatly relieved that it was not his father's voice.

Someone else shouted from the path leading to the cove and Michael knew he would have to run for it to avoid discovery. He raced into the darkness, away from the village, away from the blaze. He tripped over heather and blundered into prickly bushes, but on he went until he came to a stone wall. He scrambled over it and crouched panting on the far side. Presently he peeped over the wall and watched the flames leap from bush to bush.

"Crumbs! Even this wall won't stop it spreading," Michael exclaimed.

He watched the flames come nearer and leap ever higher, fanned by the wind. By their light he also saw men running to and fro and could hear their angry, frightened shouts.

Michael was no longer safe in his hiding place. He left it and ran further along the cliff, nearer to the sea. And that was his undoing. All unknowing,

Michael ran straight towards a wrecker who had been outposted to watch for the 'Señorita Maria' from a high vantage point. He saw Michael's fleeing form silhouetted against the flames and crouched in readiness.

"Got you, you young meddler!" he shouted, leaping out as Michael dashed past, bringing him down with a flying tackle.

CHAPTER ELEVEN

THE END OF IT ALL

Michael struggled in vain. He was held in a vice-like grip that no amount of wriggling could undo.

"What's your rotten game, you young rogue?" demanded the wrecker, trying to see Michael's face.

"Let me go! I'm trying to *stop* a rotten game, that's what," Michael panted.

"So it was you who started that fire, was it? You interferin' bounder, you'll pay dearly for your meddlin' I'll tell you. Wait till my mate Rock hears about this. He'll show no mercy, and neither should he."

It was useless trying to escape, and Michael was too puffed to run far anyway. He allowed himself to be bundled down the winding track to the beach. He tripped many times on the loose stones but the heavy hand on his collar soon pulled him to his feet again. No sooner was Michael on the beach than he was surrounded by a rabble of confused, angry men all shouting at once.

"Here's Steer, let him tell us what's up," yelled one particularly tough character.

"Thought you'd sighted the 'Señorita Maria'. What have you done with her, eh Steer?" someone else sneered.

"She's changed course and headed out to sea again," said the wrecker called Steer, "and we've got this young bounder to thank for it. Set the cliff ablaze, he did, and gave the whole show away."

The gang of rough, thwarted men pressed round more closely and Michael dreaded what would happen next. Someone lit a lantern and shone it in his face.

"Can't have been him, he's only a kid," he growled.

"It was him, you fat oaf. Saw him with my own eyes, I did," Steer declared. "A fortune's slipped through our fingers tonight, and all because this kid couldn't mind his own business. One thing's certain. He'll rue his meddlin' ways when Rock gets his hands on him."

The wreckers all shouted at once and one of them struck Michael in the face, making his nose bleed. Another clouted him round the ears and a third shook him until his brains rattled. Michael sank to the sand from fright and dizziness, only to be hauled to his feet again. And the man who dragged him up was Rock Rufus himself.

"What's going on here? And who's this kid?" he demanded.

"I caught him, guv. Set the cliff ablaze and lost us our ship, he did," Steer said. "What's best to do with a kid like that, that's what I want to know."

"What's worst you mean," Rock Rufus bellowed. "Here, Len, take this kid up the cliff and chuck him over head first."

Lobster Len pushed forward and peered into Michael's face.

"Watch it, guv. That's Mister Trevane's kid. We'd be asking for trouble if anything happened to him."

"Tie him up and dump him in our cave then," Rock Rufus ordered. "We might as well make some money out of him if we can't kill him. What say we ship him over to Flushing on our next run and sell him to our tea-bag makers? They could do with some help, the way trade's growing."

And in spite of his anger over the loss of the 'Señorita Maria', Lobster Len laughed a cruel, menacing laugh. Michael sank down again and this time he was held there while one of the men produced ropes and tied him hand and foot. Meanwhile Rock Rufus told the wreckers to disband and lie low until they heard from him again. To Michael it all seemed distant and unreal, as if it was not him who was being bound at all, and not his ears that were hearing things.

The men crunched their way off the beach, except for one who tipped Michael over his shoulder and carried him into the cave. There Michael blacked out completely.

Some time passed before Michael came round. At first he was bewildered, but the ropes biting into his wrists and ankles soon reminded him of what had happened. And here he was, the prisoner of a ruthless gang of wreckers—and of Rock Rufus in particular.

"What a mess I'm in! If only I'd stayed at home," Michael said. Then he remembered the 'Señorita Maria' and what Steer had said about her changing course.

"I saved her! I saved her!" Michael exclaimed, and a flood of joy swept over him.

He struggled to free himself, but it was no use. The harder he tried the more the ropes bit into his flesh, so he gave up and lay motionless in the darkness. How long Michael lay there he had no idea, but it was a long time. He tried to forget his plight by recalling the events of the night.

"I'm glad it wasn't me against Dad. He didn't shine that wretched lantern after all," and Michael gave a big sigh of relief.

But why hadn't he shone it? Where was he? And what was it Rock Rufus had said about tea bags? Michael's heart began to pound as he remembered more clearly.

"He said he would sell me to some bag makers in Flushing. Wherever's that? Must be in France or Brittany. He wouldn't dare! Yet what's he left me here for if he doesn't mean to come back and get me?" and Michael broke out into a sweat of fear.

"I used to be scared of Dad being transported, now it looks more like happening to me," he said.

A faint shaft of light pierced the darkness and for the first time Michael realised where he was.

"I'm in my own cave!" he whispered, and how ironical it seemed. Here he was a prisoner in the cave that had been the scene of so many of his childish, let's pretend adventures. But there was no pretence now. This was grim reality.

And then a disturbing thought came into Michael's mind and would not be pushed out.

"It sounds dreadful, but every time I've asked God to help me things have got worse," Michael whispered. And this frightened Michael more than anything else. "If God isn't on my side, I'm done," he thought, and yet how could God be on the side of wreckers? It didn't make sense.

And so Michael pondered and worried until the

shaft of light above told him it must be broad day-light outside.

"If only Rock Rufus would come. If only anything rather than lying here hour after hour," Michael said.

And yet when the longed-for sound of footsteps came, Michael all but blacked out again and his heart thumped painfully.

"Mike! Mike! Where are you?" called an anxious voice, and to his unspeakable delight it was his father who strode into the cavern.

"Oh, Dad, I thought it was that wrecker coming to export me," Michael said, his voice choked with relief. "Where've you been all this time and how did you know I was here?"

"I've been to Helston and back and a Revenue Officer told me where to find you," Mr. Trevane said, as he untied Michael's bonds.

"A Revenue Officer?"

"That's right, lad. I got to Helston without being seen by the wreckers and told everything to the magis-trate. He soon got things moving and the Revenue men arrived here as the wreckers were making their way to the Downs. A fight broke out and some of the wreckers escaped, but the Officers got Rock Rufus and Lobster Len. It was Lobster Len who let on about you. I suppose he thought he would get off more lightly if he turned helpful."

"God knew it would be best to let things get worse and worse until those moonshiners were caught," Michael blurted out. "And there was me doubting whether He'd even heard my prayers."

"So we have God to thank for all this, have we?" his

father said reverently. "I hope it's not too late for Him to forgive a backslider like me."

"It's never too late," Michael shouted triumphantly, and how good life suddenly seemed.

"Let's get away, lad. We've both seen more than enough of this cave," said his father.

Michael tried to stand but wobbled badly.

"Ouch, my feet are all pins and needles," he complained. So Mr. Trevane picked him up and carried him into the daylight.

And to Michael it seemed so right that the wind had dropped and the sun was shining once more.

Back home, Mum wrapped Michael in a warm blanket and gave him a mug of hot milk to drink. Never had milk tasted so delicious.

Later that day Michael's Uncle Arthur and Trevor came over. All Helston buzzed with the news of the wreckers' capture, but Uncle Arthur was only concerned for the welfare of his brother and nephew.

"It's all over, I'm clear of smuggling for good," Mr. Trevane said. "I feel like a new man already, thank God."

"We must indeed thank God," his brother agreed warmly.

"Mike, you remember John Wesley, don't you?" Trevor asked.

"Of course I do."

"Well, he's staying with us again next week and he'd like to preach in this village. Will you spread it around that he's coming?"

"Rather!" Michael said.

And so John Wesley did come and almost the whole

village turned out to hear him. It was a day never to be forgotten and many learned for the first time that God loved them and had sent His Son to die for them.

"Whatever your sin, it's not too late to turn to God for forgiveness," Mr. Wesley told them, and many villagers found new life and joy by doing just that. Michael too was glad that he had asked for God's forgiveness, that day on the Downs.

Some weeks later the squire of that part of Cornwall called on the Trevanes and told them of his plan to have a lighthouse built to warn passing ships of the treacherous Devil's Teeth.

"It has been suggested to me that you, as a local man, should quarry the stones for my project, Mr. Trevane. Are you willing, my good man?" the squire asked airily.

And Mr. Trevane assured him he would be only too pleased.

"I'd be glad to do anything to rid our coast of shipwrecks," he said.

And it astounded Michael the number of people who crossed the Goonhilly Downs to visit the village in days to come. It became all but a sightseeing resort since the notorious Rock Rufus was captured there—and a local boy averted a shipwreck by setting the cliff on fire.

As there was no place where they could worship God together, the villagers decided to rebuild the ruined chapel. And Michael's father was asked to quarry the granite for this as well. When the little chapel was finished, the Trevanes were among the happy people who worshipped God there.